the
THREE
JEWELS

the THREE JEWELS

A Modern Myth

NIRMALA NATARAJ

WINGED SERPENT PRESS

Winged Serpent Press
New York

Copyright © 2023 by Nirmala Nataraj. All rights reserved.

All images by Slobodan Dan Paich. Reprinted with permission.

All rights reserved. No part of this publication may be reproduced, stored in a retrieval system or transmitted in any form or by any means (electronic, mechanical, photocopying, recording, or otherwise) without the written permission of the author and publisher.

Paperback ISBN: 979-8-9870309-0-5
eBook ISBN: 979-8-9870309-1-2
Library of Congress Control Number: 2022921570

Book cover and interior design by Erin Seaward-Hiatt

Editorial production by kn literary

For Slobodan, who shared the magic of his vision over many cups of tea and conversations imbued with cosmic knowledge.

ANY MOONS AGO, there was a woman—or was she only half woman? Sometimes she felt like a little girl; other times she felt like a wizened old crone; and yet other times she felt like something altogether alien, something without organs or humors or the slightest tendency to leave a sign of its passage — even waste or sorrow — as living ones are wont to do.

The story was so old it was easy to mis-remember, or at least momentarily misplace — even for the one at the very center of it.

She walked in darkness for a long time, in a place where the memory of light was as murky as the moldering walls and the pools of sludge that paved the path ahead of her. Darkness reached across the horizon like a pair of arms from a watery grave. It had been like this for so long, not that it mattered . . . for this was a place where the very blinking tinkering thought of time was without essence.

Indeed, how long it had been like this, she was not entirely sure. And even certainty, in the end, had lost its power of persuasion, when all was prayed and done.

She remembered very little, except, only vaguely, a time when the garden was overgrown with weeds and shadows, when hope gave way to the sweet wreckage of reminiscence and love became a melody in a music box that was forever frozen shut, impervious to meddlesome eyes.

A heart is something that must be protected from interlopers, even if that requires forgetting, she would tell herself over and over again. *Even if I imagined the whole thing, I know there is something in me that is willing to stare into the mouth of death, to face the ruins alone if need be.*

The woman walked slowly through the deep, abyssal always-night, fearful yet resolute. She wore an elaborate casement of armor whose origins might have been hinted at in just the right light, but that had been long forgotten — a dubious booty. Although she wore it as if it had never *not* been a part of her, she knew only that it protected her from the darkness, which had once not been such a formidable adversary.

Although she was sure that it was not *of* her, she could not recall a time when this armor didn't settle around her like a halo of gathered dreams, a second skin as close and intimate as the air she breathed. Dense as a soldier's livery, it was caked with fish scales, strewn with odd bits of tusk and hardened earth and corroded metal and the fangs of unknown beasts, netted together with the gravity of an Apocryphal chant. No chinks in this armor, no. A masterwork forged by the bellows of a craftsman infatuated with his tools, this beauty was assembled with painstaking patience and unlikely glee.

And my memory rises up and out like a pair of hands from the grave, clasped around my neck, as the cold lips of the corpse draw closer and closer to my face. The kiss of death . . . a seduction that will always be with me, that keeps me going . . .

She walked for what seemed to be light years, and by some quick instinct, she knew the ancientness of the places her feet trod upon. Places between shadow and light, action and response, as primeval as exile.

In this place, ghosts lingered. Here, every word that had ever been uttered, every thought ever believed, every task unfinished, every god that had expired into the fog of oblivion just because someone, many ones, had stopped believing.

Here, in this place, in the overgrown moss and the cold, hard earthen walls, a stolen memory rustled ever so softly.

Here, in this place, there were not simply phantoms but other beings, the kind that watch and wait and make themselves known only through whispers, or vague imprints of cool fire on the flesh, or the occasional snaky limb of a tree whose roots twine up from the earth, or the waft of a familiar odor, or a song whose tune's been heard countless time but can't be placed.

Yes, she was a warrior not wholly impassive to the sinister summons of the land, which

belted out its cri de coeur for blood sacrifice. Her armor, clunky and clangorous as it was, was the only reliable talisman against the age-old suffering of this place. Here, in the hinterlands between realms, where spirits looked on with the unaffected knowledge that even decay has its mortality.

She was compelled by her own nature and by the circumstances at hand to be slow, as the armor that shuttered her limbs made her passage awkward and nearly painful. Her helmet weighed her down, shading her eyes from the already dusky land, darkened by the distant glow of planets that shone tremulously in the heavens.

But, most peculiar, only when she closed her eyes was her vision illuminated by a faint blue umbra that filled her with a slight warmth, vibrated her bones, and set her ablaze with determination that seemed not entirely her own. Only the light behind her eyes gave her the strength to trundle along.

As she walked, the spirits around her whirled in silent expectation, alive and facelessly aware, like reeds in a field, bowing apart to make way for the approaching dreamer.

I am just a girl, and no more. And so I am mourning a virginity that was taken from me prematurely—seized, even. But like the women who came before me, I did not think of complaining. I suffered my plight and bit my tongue and held my head high even though everything in me was descending to a long and slow point miles beneath my feet, in a place where everything halted to a lack, a dull gray absence of imagination or cheer. For so long, I must have lived that way. Is it why I set out? To see if there was even the glimmer of something good and pure and new and redeeming on the horizon—perhaps, a second innocence to bring restitution to the first one?

The world she'd journeyed from was already oceans away, and the memory of it waved about like wisps from a dream rather than a description of her life as it had existed before she was called by some unspeakable force to seek distant lands. Even the places she'd passed through just moments ago were scarcely recognizable to her. The land seemed to breathe and shift and rearrange itself like the limbs of a restless sleeping giant, which, to the diminutive observer, signaled the sudden creation of new worlds. And as the path ahead became narrow and the vines shot up like distended arms all around, it seemed to the woman that the aperture of her vision widened, and the view ahead was filmy with the largeness of the unknown.

Somewhere in the distance, she could hear the surge of water. Although she could not see its source, the ground beneath her feet began to yield and gush ever so slightly, and the cool silt of the earth shook in silken ribbons around her footprints.

Despite herself, she stopped for a moment and simply stood, her feet sinking pleasurably like rocks planting into the suckling undertow.

As she walked farther and farther, the water pooled around her, whispering at her ankles and rising against her limbs. And as the water became higher and higher, she felt herself grow heavier and heavier. And with a sort of horror, for she knew neither the span nor depth of the body she had entered, she understood that if she were to continue, her armor would have to come off.

If I do not free myself from the weight of the known, I will be too heavy. If I am too heavy, I will sink. If I sink, I will disappear, and the world will be none the worse, none the better. But can I do what must be done?

Removing her armor, slowly, painfully, felt like peeling off a tough, dense scab that seemed more real than the tender veins that tensed and contracted beneath its stalwart protection.

This was armor that boasted every-thing from the rough-hewn skins of extinct creatures whose deadly cadaverous dance across her flesh made her feel the reaches of her own madness, almost triumphantly. The armor included everything from the iridescent scales of undersea dragons to the plumage of a phoenix molting on the cusp of its airborne rebirth. The armor was linked by everything from the silken pelt of a jaguar to the crystalline shards of a unicorn's horn. The armor was littered with everything from the taut gossamer of a fairy's dress to the delicate wrinkled petals of a rose in its fullest and most fertile bloom. The armor was bound by innumerable blessings and curses, by indescribable sorrows and travails, glittering boons and lingering regrets tamped in place by the wafer-thin skin of a wicked witch who had come to a corrupt and lonely end.

Everything on the gods' green earth could be found in this armor, ground into a shimmering mesh yet still bursting with the bloated fancies of past lives and destined futures. There was the thumb of a dwarf that had been bitten off in a skirmish with a sea serpent, whose wavy dark tentacles still trembled beneath the rotting blue-black nail. And there was the shattered, faintly luminous orb of a Nephilim's nimbus, still glowing from a fall so precipitous it could have only been from the heavens. And there was the dead eye of a poison-glutted basilisk, encrusted within the frozen gullet of a Gorgon.

How painful removing the armor felt to her! She could sense the blood flowing in her veins, despite the cool air on her skin. Her blood seared like hellfire within her, as if it gushed from open wounds, although the only wounds she bore were metaphysical.

As the armor came off, little by little, the land around her began to assume discernible shape and form. A beam of light issued suddenly from her skin as she looked around, beholding the new world that had suddenly sprouted at her feet like a lotus risen from a previously impenetrable promontory of mud. A single arrow of light shot out from her body, circling it delicately until she was cushioned by an orb of fire.

She was not alarmed at this new turn of events. It was wonderful, really. She didn't know if it was coming from her, or if the radiance that flooded in and out was simply the effect of her bodily sensations rushing into the void the armor had left in its absence. She drank in this newfound freedom, the milky wash of vision that splashed over her.

Dunes rose over the horizon, purple mounds in the shaky distance. A pinkish aureole of air settled and sighed lazily around. Gem-ensconced rock formations sprawled out in all directions, and caves bubbled out from their heights — yawning whorls of mouths that seemed to alternately smile and grimace. This place, which had appeared so sinister, so treacherous, just moments before, was now imbued with an eerie grace. Even the echoes of ghostly whispers were like the lazily strung-together notes of a forest orchestra. Why, she wondered, had she not noticed before? And yet . . . why was it all so familiar, as if she had been jostled awake only by the presence of her body, of a tangible self?

She waded into a widening pool of water; dark liquid gurgled over the shale and made her slip on the smooth rocks.

Something — like the abrupt crinkle of a smooth sheet of paper — flashed across her peripheral vision. That thing that moved noiselessly nearby popped like a fat bubble in her memory. She closed her eyes, and a

fizzy bulb flashed upon a scene that was just as vivid as any dream she'd summoned from the ethers.

There she was, in the midst of a deep green meadow, far from the cold, hard monotony of the land she had come from. Could this be a vision from her childhood? It seemed so unlikely and so far away. But here it was, touchable and solid and *here*. Verdant earth and fresh cool air all around that she drank deeply, as if it would be her sole foray from this subterranean cavern. Fir trees and poplars and daffodils and chrysanthemums — the smell and sight of them filled the velvet air.

Sacred, sacred, everything sacred! Empires are lain waste, and the world goes on, but there is only one dark endless road that runs alongside life, that is always on a parallel path, even as we forge ahead in blissful ignorance. Please, gods, don't let it be a cruel trick. Let me buy a bit of this time that has bent itself backward for my amusement!

As she took in the sights and sounds around her, she suddenly felt three pebbles surface beneath her bare feet. They were peculiarly complex — extraordinarily faceted and luminous. As she picked them up and peered more closely into each, she could see entire worlds revolving within the gems, in mutual symmetrical orbits. Not worlds, even, but dimensions with a myriad of details and doorways into different fates, set like whirling eyes within the stones.

Each angle of each stone was cut to a precise calculation. A menagerie of shapes flitted across the glassy crystals. Beings as strange and full and self-contained as the earth herself when one stopped to regard her as an entire being. Entities with inordinate power and karmic cycles that entwined with hers, while having, simultaneously, nothing whatsoever to do with her.

She saw many things she didn't understand: images within images that were puzzles whose edges she had yet to apprehend with her eyes, fingers, senses. But if she threw the jewels, just so, at such an angle that their secrets poured out like darkening suns into lunar oceans, perhaps she could see further, past the miniature doors that had been opened. Perhaps she could catch the mutating bolts of light before they dove, reckless and free and unheeding of her, into the seductive and watery depths!

Am I to know you? Am I to see something more than strange gliding undines across the surface of a faraway mirror?

And just like that, the vague horizon of her sight exploded into color. Into a story, a picture, a place, a definite where. Yes! *Here!* Here was a tree that was really a girl, a young girl as sturdy as a birch, who stood on the lip of a dune at the edge of her own jewel world, providing shade to journeyers who had reached the very frontiers of their lives and now wondered if there was anything more to see or be astounded by. Oh, how sad were her branches, weighted down by the groaning winds and the chasms of stars that emptied from the sky. The woman turned away from the vision. It was too much, too much!

Another lightning crack . . . and just over there! A dark swirl of petals enfolding a soft sylph of a woman, her face encircled by a halo of raven curls, her eyes bright pools of intense shadow. A lady of secrets, a keeper of obsessions that drive sentient beings to desperate ends. This lady was a water-drenched lotus rising from a desert of scorched hope, a sweet wisp of knowledge in the midst of a blank and still void, a ladder of fire rising from a dull life, a gray life, an inner world reduced to rubble and ash. Like the sweet fragrance of a flower that blooms only in the loneliest hour of night, when the voices of humans and spirits alike are silenced by anticipation, this beautiful woman circled up and out from the blackest of worlds like a rope of hands reaching toward the firmament. She was a being both celestial and chthonic.

And here! Half man and half ibis, wings folded in until they were hard shining projectiles pointed at the earth, ready to take flight. Oh, the wisdom that silhouetted this walker of realms, who seemed to boil in the midst of half-seen visions, half-visioned realities. Yes, a place that few people had ever known. A reality beyond reality — *that* was the place where this one stayed. And it was a place to which the woman, so brave in her ignorance, had never traveled, but which she knew could be reached, quickly now, on a velvet wind that breathes through the open eyes of a cloudless day. Such are the sojourns on which invisible wings can sweep you so briskly. Clear and dreamless places where a shy tune resounds.

All this before my eyes: old visions torn asunder, and new ones borne aloft; radiance replaced by broken shells; broken shells replaced by new life.

What are *you?* she asked in a language that resembled nothing she had ever said or heard. She clutched at herself in dumb amazement upon hearing the sound that floated from her. Was she really capable of *that* voice? She spoke in glyphs that reverberated like something avowed under water. Her syllables were gurgles, winding out like scarves untangling from her throat. Had it really been so long since she had spoken? Her voice, which had perhaps at some point been such an exalted instrument, a sparrow song, a kiss in color, a puff of perfumed air, was as awkward to her as her former body. Her armored body.

When they responded, it was not in the tongue she consciously heard when she spoke to herself, in a voice so porous and moist and faint that it seemed to waft from the moss on the hard walls she had once dragged her fingers across.

No, the words of these entities were forged by the bellows of divine rage — hot, blue, and spitting forth webs of urgent flame.

We heard you call us, they said, the words echoing in some dragon-guarded part of her brain. *Even though you didn't make so much as a sound. You tore into the veils that separate the worlds, and your cry flew across the nearest wastelands and farthest paradises. And we heard you.*

She could not understand, yet none of it was a surprise. They went on and on, taking her through cycles of time and story, through twilights of gods from pantheons she had never known existed. Wasn't the time of the gods dead, after all? Hadn't it existed only in some distant girlhood whose vestiges were as ashen as the hills around her were green — a memory that sang through unseen throats the song of a tale yet to be?

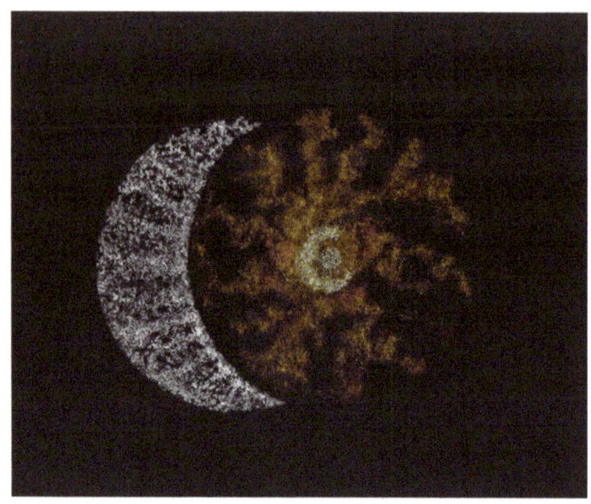

The time of our time has come to its end, but because you called to us, and because we need you, we have come to you now, they continued.

When did I call to you? Was it when I walked the tunnel with my heavy armor and yearned for torchlight? You did not come then. Did you hear me?

Yes, we heard you. But that wasn't when you called.

When did I call to you? Was it when I removed my garments and revealed my naked flesh to the demons that surrounded me, no doubt wishing to feast upon my disgrace? You did not come then. Did you hear me?

Yes, we heard you. But that wasn't when you called.

When did I call to you? Was it when I was so starved for food and for the company of others that I dug up handfuls of earth to fill my mouth and blot out the memory of tender hands upon my body? You did not come then. Did you hear me?

Yes, we heard you. But that wasn't when you called.

When did I call to you? Was it when I was forced to battle enemies seen and unseen, without a weapon or an army to carry me to victory? You did not come then. Did you hear me?

Yes, we heard you. But that wasn't when you called.

When did I call to you? Was it when I was cast out by my brethren and given nothing for comfort but a dark path surrounded by treacherous wayfarers and the constant presence of death? You did not come then. Did you hear me?

Yes, we heard you. But that wasn't when you called.

Speak to me, then! I have no other memories. And if you did not hear me in my time of need, you are as good as useless to me!

You sowed the seeds of our arrival not in your time of need but in the time when you had no need other than to give freely of yourself.

Abruptly, the voices ceased and she was jolted back into herself, an exhausted soul falling upon the hard earth, as if it were a bed of feathers. And what flashed into her consciousness was both old and new, cursed and consecrated: the story of herself that she had willed into oblivion. And as it was seen and heard and told and remembered, something more than a phantom from her dreaming past came to sit beside her, watchfully.

The young girl strewed petals from a basket of daisies that she'd just picked at the farthest peaks of the mountain, where its blue shadow stood steadfastly against the approaching prow of the land. Yes, *that* mountain, the one that spired up from the earth and into a cool spiral of clouds. Another forbidden place she had scaled with no hesitation. She was proud of her courage; hers was a pride that emerged from naked innocence rather than desire.

She had lived in the valley just over the bluff all her life, for thrice fifty moons, much longer than she could count. But despite the admonitions that had been beaten into her by

her gods-fearing parents, despite the stories that had filled her imaginings since she was just a wee one, she was not afraid. In fact, she believed that she was the only one who knew anything of the vast expanses beyond the confines of her cave-dwelling brethren — from the dizzying heights of the mountain to the bone-strewn red dirt of the battlefield beyond the valley. And as lovely as the former place was, with its dew-drenched ravines and grassy capes and cavorting clouds and spumes of falling water, she had always been more entranced by that desolate, shorn field below, where the playful lust of the seasons had been quelled by the wrath of the Old Ones. Nothing grew there.

When she first glimpsed it, she knew she'd be beaten one inch from death if her people ever found out. And all the same, she knew it was her duty to bring those mountain flowers, so opalescent and delicate and breathtakingly of this moment, down to the dread place. This place, where ancient ghouls howled their hatred of the living to the ones who still had ears to hear with. She was old enough to stay silent about her whereabouts but young enough to be unafraid. They used to visit her in the night, and while others had miscalculated their guttural yelps as clear signs of warning—perhaps clear enough to move the entire village westward, away from the craggy rock and toward the sun-dappled ocean—she was not dissuaded. She knew, not knowing how she knew, that the ghosts were not embittered by hatred but by loneliness.

As she hummed a low tune, she sprinkled the soil with her blossoms, which were still wet with dew. How faintly they glowed against the dark, suffering earth! She bent to admire them, her breath catching in her throat at the unexpected puddle of tears pooling on

the blooms. She stood, brushing away the

salty stream flooding out of her. As she walked

along, the winds blew about like wild mares

or the curses of bodiless spirits, forcing her

to cover her face with her dress. She knew

that the specters detested her for her plump

limbs and her light-filled eyes that could yet

perceive, but she did not begrudge them this.

Perhaps she would have felt the same had she

been forced to live out eternity in such a waste-

land. So as they screamed their obscenities,

which would have rattled any intrepid soul, she simply kept her eye on the sea of flowers that she spread before her, likening them to stars, as the burnished glow of the sun became fainter and fainter.

"You are me, I am you, and we are one," she began to sing the tune that she was humming, without a clear idea of where the words had come from. Had they ever not been a part of her? "You are me, I am you, we are one, and love is the law of the land."

To think of it—love the law of *this* land? This land, with its peril spelled out in the countless white bones that littered the path ahead of her in an alphabet arrangement of some dead language? How precisely the remains had been laid upon the earth, mirroring the great conjunction that the Old Ones had predicted eons ago. The great conjunction that would wipe out all those who had ever lived and died, so that all, babes and rheumy-eyed uncles alike, would face a fate as wretched as these poor fools who had fought tooth and nail for . . . what? An already bereft ideal, since no one remembered it. Or perhaps not an ideal, but an idea as forgettable as the wheel marks of the caravans that would amble through her village every now and then. Rutted grooves in the dusty road would eventually succumb to nature. How could her little heart not be swayed by mercy . . . as well as the dawning dream, perhaps nothing more than a wish at that point, that the law of the Old Ones was deserving of sacrilege?

"Love is the law of this land! Love is the law of this land!" she intoned almost zealously. The incantation that had come from nowhere, or all wheres, pervaded her entire being. The flowers she tossed upon the ground appeared to multiply before her eyes. Adorned as they were by the blooms, the bones were no longer bleached spearheads of death, but beautiful armaments, like the branches of pale trees that support the burgeoning-forth of life.

She felt a lightness in her body as she spanned the vast terrain and dropped her flowers, which continued to replenish themselves naturally so that she never ran out. On and on she went like this, despite the whispers that gnawed at her feet and hated her lithe gait. Yet she abided, until even those malefic murmurs stilled to a drowsy silence.

This little one, who had been forbidden by the denizens of her tribe to pay homage to the damned spirits who roamed this land — proud and defeated self-same — had surpassed the remotest wishes and hopes of the dead, gone well beyond their expectations. Suffering and sacrifice, a meaningful offering to quell the revenants who slept with eyes wide awake, were the only things they'd ever thought to ask for — or rather, demand. But this gesture was so unabashed and gentle, unlike anything they'd considered revering or requesting from the dreamers who lived. What was it that made them still, so that they could only watch her in sullen wonder as she made her shimmering orbit around the necropolis, with those pale flowers raining grace upon their remnants?

On and on she went, uttering her incantation, which filled her with lightness and grace so that she thought she would be made breathless, a mere gale on the wind, by her weird joy. On and on she went, until the sky turned a purple-rose and the falcons cresting overhead swooped back to their mountain retreats. On and on she went, until the air was chilled by the remaining clouds, darkened yet warmed by the lingering flames of the sun. And that battleground, previously so stark and uninviting, was a field of fluffy cream upon which starlings alighted. On and on she went, almost delirious in the wake of her beauty-making. Nobody had taught the young girl beauty, not even her foremothers, whose harsh faces were lined by the ravages of sun and squalor. Nobody in her village knew beauty, only the unchanging cycles of starvation, toil, necessity.

On and on she went, and the sky became darker still. On and on she went, and the once-clamoring spirits became quiet, attentive, protective even, of their curious visitor. On and on she went . . . until the clocktower in the valley behind the bluff struck its deafening knell. Only then did the girl startle and gaze toward the land of her brethren. Only then did she realize that her covert activities would remain so no longer. Only then did her heart swell and shrink at the idea of her impending punishment.

And only then did she become impervious to all suffering but her own.

❦

At this point, the details of her sacrilege, trial, and exile came to her only in lightning-quick bolts of image and sound. The echoes of children's malicious laughter on the far side of the bluff as they looked down upon her strange ritual with the knowledge that she would have to answer to the Old Ones' laws . . . a welt across the side of her face, where her mam had slapped her so hard she had fallen like a sack of turnips upon the dirt floor of the hut . . . a single wild red rose upon her family's door, ringed in white chalk, to signify the transgression . . . the wails and lamentations of the womenfolk, made more dramatic against the silence of her own family . . . the black shadows of the Old Ones' long wizened faces in the hall that housed the clocktower . . . the ice in her veins upon their pronouncement. The High Councilor placed his thumb upon her forehead, and between her eyes she felt a cold shiver that shot into her skull. This was the mark of the tainted—the mark placed on the one who came to know things they should never have come to know.

"From now on, you will no longer be called by name or be recognized by kin or those other savage races who roam the hinterlands beyond the Valley of the Fearing Folk. You will be cast out for your treachery, ever to taste only its poison as your sole nourishment. You will be clothed by the meager coverings you have upon you, bathed only by your tears, kept alive by whatever warmth your breath shall muster. Those who remain in fear upon this earth will have naught to do with you, as they will know that yours is the path of the damned. You will expire in unknown lands, prey to beasts and savages—your maidenhood violated, your bones gnashed and mutilated, for the sign of the wicked shall be upon you until your flesh is lain to rest and your spirit is made to wander the wastes in search of a door that will never open to you. All this have we seen, and all this is yet to come."

Upon their judgment, just as the clock struck high noon, the villagers followed her in near silence to the outskirts just beyond the boneyards, where mangy mutts circled the grounds in search of a scrap of fallen meat. They yelped excitedly, ropes of saliva swinging from their bared fangs, when they caught sight of the procession. Surely, another sack of

flesh was to be added to the blackened heap! But her fate would not be so quickly meted out. The oldest of the Old Ones, a violet-robed hunchback with curdled gray eyes and a voice as wobblesome as his chin, stepped forward and silenced the muttering crowd with an upraised arm.

"Brethren, today we send forth this gods-forsaken child into the black unknown of her fate. May whatever spirits who stoop to take pity on her be moved, and may our village be kept in their custody by virtue of our fear."

At that, all averted their eyes and walked back to the village, stiff as stone—faces hollow and expressionless, given the order that blasphemous tears shed for the exiled be punishable by labor in the boneyards. She wanted to run after them and beg mercy, but to follow them would have been to seal her own tomb, for disobedience of the Old Ones' edicts was tantamount to death. Only one person, a boy with whom she had once woven daisy chains at the Steeple of Arms close to the foothills she'd loved so much, glanced back with forlorn eyes before he covered his face with his hands and walked off.

And then what happened? the three jewels asked in unison.

She paused and communicated her story through her mind's eye, as she had done with the desultory compilation of memories that had come flooding back to her. She now recalled her treks through distant lands, and how she had initially marked time by scrying the waning belly of the Great Mother in the Sky. She recalled the manner in which she had braved wild, remote kingdoms, the manner in which she had been abused by beasts and men alike — most of whom eventually shied away from her,

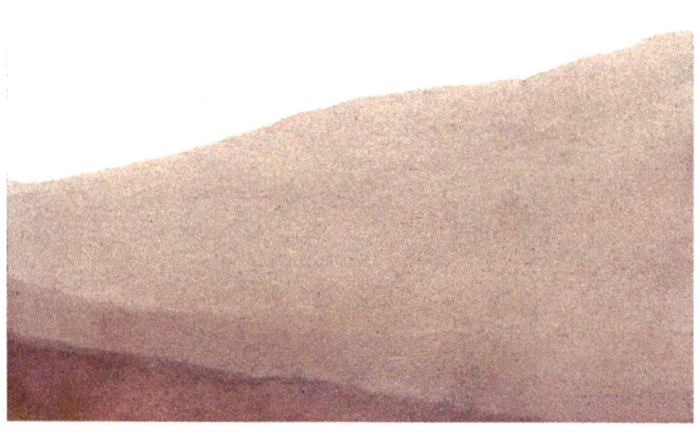

as it was considered taboo to touch the one who
bore the mark of the exiled. She recalled the
random bits of mesh, netting, lost booty, and
unearthly offal that she'd scavenged from boneyards and caves of worship to form her protective armor. She recalled the mer-cold tremble in
her flesh, which nearly compelled her to throw
herself upon flaming pyres or into chthonic
burial grounds, or to wish herself impaled on
the talons of a bird of prey, only to be dissuaded
by the watery thing in her bowels that was

older than fear. Of course, thieving from caves of worship only added insult to injury, but she had never nursed much faith in the gods—and now, the edicts of the Old Ones had hardened her heart to such nonsense altogether and eternally. She recalled the diaphanous smoky outlines of the spirits of the fallen, who gathered around her not simply out of a sense of duty to this lone wanderer, whose ruin had come at the hands of a dubious tribunal, but out of curiosity for what would eventually become of her. Many kalpas spent in their own incorporeal exile had confirmed for them the greatness that was attained in due time for those living ones who were made to rove and create their homes and birth their offspring in foreign lands.

And what to say of that child? What to make of that child? Who was she now, and what was anyone's business with her? She, who had traveled a tenuous path, as if she were a spider folding in on her own convex trajectory, had unfurled and widened the spiral, only to find herself collapsing back upon it—or unraveling it all to enter a netherworld, a dreamed and dreaming world, in which the longings of the insensate self could be given voice. What was the lesson to be learned here, if she could find the strength to scavenge a lesson at all from the detritus of her past?

The three jewels responded to the question she could not yet voice. *You carry sorrow with you, but know that your desire to shine upon the pain of others your curious grace was the one thing that saved you from succumbing to death or the countless trickster gods.*

And still, and still . . . what had any of this to do with her? The one with the sad gazelle eyes, and the one with wings the span of apocalypse, and the one with arms weighted

down with bursting, ripe, forgotten fruit — all
stepped forth in unison and sang themselves
into her bones so that she was filled with the
whirl and heft of them, like a wind entering
her most delicate spaces, undeniably. And
the violation was pure and pleasant torture,
as it was the closest she had come to being
touched — truly *touched* — in all the moments of
her exile.

The worlds in which we abided so long became
worn around the edges, and they will die soon. But
we can be reborn into a new world that is bereft of
gods except in word and ritual alone. You called out
to us and we heard you. And if you bring us in, new
possibilities shall be birthed for the inauspicious.
The arcana of the Dream Hermits has attested to
this. For we were the guardians of those who sought
egress to the Overworld. Those who have roamed the
lands in search of escape and relief will no longer
be captives in the purgatory of the living. You will

*be tasked with building temples for the new gods,
as well as for the wandering dead. You shall restore
faith to the faithless, placate the suffering among
the dead, and build new roads for the living.*

At this, she smarted. Temples built to honor the gods, as well as the dead? The long

shadow of her misfortune had made her shun both the gods and the dead. What good had they been to her, in her exile?

Before the cataract of bitterness could spew from her mouth, the jeweled ones passed through her once more so that her pain could be redirected like a vein of tree sap, viscous and sweet, into the spaces within their embrace, rather than uttered. For, as we all know, every utterance has a falling place where it is seeded and sprouts into its own bedizened reality. All the same, one half-believed sentiment was siphoned from that forsaken cesspool: *The gods are dead to me.*

In perfumed clouds of rose and incense, the wraiths rose around her, trembling across the mirage of her sadness.

Radiant one, the gods don't die; they are simply reborn in more hospitable places, or those lands that are so parched and empty of hope that the void creates a desire. In this land, we will not be reborn in slender towers reaching toward the empyrean, or as colossal monoliths holding eternal flames beaconing a false message of peace and goodwill. We will not be reborn as beings or ideas, but as memories of that which has always been part of you.

Again, the world from which she came, ragged and yellow with age, took shape on the horizon of her last twinkling thoughts, dressed anew in the finery of the dispossessed, which made her feel as if she held, with a gingerly grasp, a treasured tome spilling out from aged leather. Had she known, all those years ago, that she would be pushed to the very cusp of her endurance in the effort to set that world free from its prejudices? That world, so gray and cold and lifeless (even in its denial of death)—had she even loved it? Was love a part of her, or was it a distant siren song that skimmed the waters of a place older, more rarefied, than memory?

But of course, it hadn't always been like this—tribe against tribe, neighbor against neighbor, legions of Old Ones silencing the tender words of lovers with their ugly premonitions and a quick warning flourish of the index finger. This world, which had become a mirror of hulking shadows, had once bloomed with roses and boughs of willow, with marble

temples girdled in fruit and blond goblets. Before the wars, which had blotted out sunlight with beasts of burden and munitions, her land was verdant and fertile and unashamed. Myths flowed darkly from the stone, like milk or wine. Colossal birds traced a path to bronze icons whose fecund centers were concealed by sprays of fruit, made as offerings by those who still sought the gods' favor.

Yes, she remembered hearsay of that brave and lively world, in which songs of shivering wheat were sung by women in white (mourners, perhaps?) and ocean-bound priestesses made rituals alongside the receding shorelines. Vendors of exotic delectables and soothsayers peddling forgotten truths shared neighboring booths in the marketplace. The sinews of men were contorted in valor rather than torture or exhaustion. Women adorned their hips with wreaths of myrrh and rubbed

beet juice on their lips. Drunken youths bayed at the moon, that blundering, beautiful orb. There was music—oh, there was *such* music!

But then came the days of the stern and angry clouds that rained down their sulfur and brimstone, the days of shattered colonnades and broken idols, the days of the Old Ones. The gods had been known to create trouble, to insert unpredictable desires into the contemplations of forest hermits, but for all their mischief, without them the world became one of solemnity, hair shirts, and abandoned lyres. No more was there music in the marketplace or brightly colored banners adorning poles on festival days. Vanity had become the sin punishable by death, the sin that made small bands of scared men and women cluster together in their dark caves and mountain alcoves. Those who were not driven by fear were driven by the torment of rage. They were impelled by some horrible rune to march forth to the far corners of the world where the sun beat high upon unforgiving earth, clanging their javelins. Some seasonal shift had brought with it an ungodly zephyr, blown in from icy and remote gullies with little room or patience for the budding things of spring. Perhaps there were faint remnants of gods in the majestic poses of trees or mountains, but the dryads and gnomes had retreated altogether. After all was said and done, the gods had fled — or died. Life was a sheet of shirred black night that lacked the grace of cosmic darkness. Everything was flat and opaque.

Is there any way out of this?

Her question was less a question than a solemn renunciation of the endless moons of shoeless wandering that had led her to this place. The mere thought of a conclusion to her suffering seemed absurd, but still, the death of this simple hope was too cruel a prospect to bear.

You have already found a way out. The aureoles of light whispered and winked like wise witch-women.

I do not understand, she importuned.

The sacred is that which must not be transgressed; that which, if you transgress it, violates your relationship to society. Sacrifice redeems society. Your sacrifice was brought about because you had the fore-sight, which was heedless of consequence at the time, to remember those whose journey to the Overworld would not be blessed, due to your people's superstition. To remember one with love, even if you did not know them, is the highest form of consecration imagin-able. It surpasses time; it transcends the small and measly injunctions of humans. In order for the soul to journey to other places, it must be remembered in this way. Your act of courage as a little one enabled the spirits whom you blessed to be reborn in auspicious places, not because they were deserving, but because you graced them with your mourning and recognized your kinship. Thus, your destiny has always been one of coming to the end of the road, where everything takes shape as a spiral and nothing ever truly dies.

From the vantage point of a nest rest-ing atop a narrow peak, she could see her world upon the brink of collapse. What she saw came to her upon plumes of smoky violet

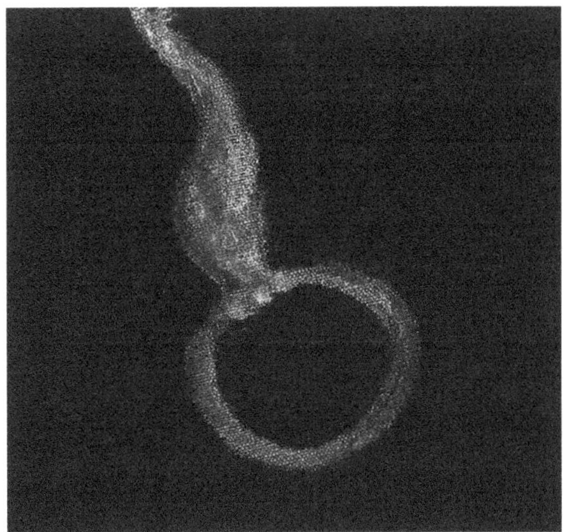

incense, upon clouds of ash and fire. Far, far

below, she could see a fork in a mud-rutted

road — one side leading to a glen cloaked

in darkness and mist, the other drooping

sadly into a volcanic pit of death and prayers

uttered too late; hands and limbs twitched

and melted in the inferno, the desperate

screams of babes and grannies alike joined by

the gleeful screech of Pandemonium itself.

She could not cry out. Her throat was choked by the fumes of this subtle vision, and by a fear greater than anything she had ever experienced. This lesser world, the one that was already enclosed in the flames of apocalypse, was one she had never been a citizen of, and so it was not exactly loss that she felt. And that other world, the one some part of her longed for because it was so far from this one, the world shrouded in nocturnal secrecy and the wayward fantasies of any well-meaning imbecile who has not yet seen life for what it is, was not exactly enticing, not exactly idyllic. After all, idylls are the lands not of wayfaring strangers but of those who are deaf to the thrush-song of human suffering.

You have a choice here, at last. The voices of the three jewels were hands passing through clouds, holding out goblets of fire and brimstone, of glass and reflection.

I can't . . . I can't. Finally, the cry in her throat broke like a cloud clapped by thunder.

The end of the world you've known is the beginning of the world to come. That is the way it has always been, for gods and mortals alike. All eventually returns to its source.

The vision before her became more and more haphazard, more and more dire. And yet the fire that danced around her was joyful and spry, not demonic and bent on destruction, as she might have guessed.

All suffering is an illusion when you view it in the midst of fire, the jeweled ones uttered. *Even the perils that darkness grants you are gifts when you see them through newborn eyes.*

She could not give her answer as she gazed upon the black shadows that lay between the two roads below—which led to two different possibilities. That mysterious force that willed into existence creation and destruction alike made the very prospect of consolation almost laughable. This was what *was*, and nothing could be anything other than it. Neither choice — plunging into the inferno or voyaging to a reality that was still in its embryonic stages — felt satisfying.

This world that had spit her forth was one of timeless wars, endless bloodshed. What was the meaning of the epoch in which she breathed and in which she would eventually expire? Nothing could endure. It was a world in which civilizations came and went, as easily as the wind. It was a world of terror, joy, awe, suspense — in which the dwellers of the numinous, of the invisible, were hidden at all times.

This was the hell realm of the gods, in whose magic all of creation was concentrated. Admission was granted to the brave few, those who might be able to hold the tension of the future without the succor of future reward. It was unbearable.

Finally, she cried out. *Please, please, if you are gods, then let me die!* Funny, she had never thought about death in any real way before, even in the times she'd found herself groveling in roadside trenches flooded with piss and garbage, because these were the safest places in which to take cover from marauders and other violent itinerants. But now, standing before these beautiful wraiths, she thought that at least death would be a more graceful, a more dignified, departure — possibly, even a painless one. She no longer had grand visions of a life after life, of the supposedly sapphire-studded staircases that rose up through the Hall of Dreams, which, as a wee one, she would conjure in her mind's eye. A blanket of warmth and blackness. The erasure of concepts such as "hot" and "cold." Freedom from thinking or knowing or wondering. If that was death, there could be nothing sweeter.

Why? Do you think you are incapable of bearing the vision of what is to come? Do you think you are the sole bearer of the vision, never to escape its burden? You are the mother of a race of new gods. We are the riddles you are meant to protect, to treasure, to bring to life. We have chosen you to be pregnant with us, to carry us into the future. If you refuse this instant, you will never experience the absolution you seek. For salvation is not in the next world. You know this already.

Somewhere beyond the green, green fields, she could see the grotesque wet innards of the tunnel through which she'd magically emerged. She saw a tower on a dune. A mist above embryonic depths. If she squinted her eyes in just the correct way, she could see into those depths . . . and there, the three jewels were gleaming. They appeared to be here, everywhere, nowhere.

How do I bring you into this world?

You must trust us.

What must I do?

Come close and you will see.

She walked closer to the apparitions, closer and closer until they were simply blurs on the edge of time, blips in the clouds— hardly solid, hardly there.

A tree of hands. A mouth of petals. A cloak of feathers. The three emissaries were almost unreal, and as the cool sharp wind of the other world, the one whence she came, swept into the meadow of revelation, they grew more and more brittle.

Pluck us and make us real.

A wind from beyond the veils of this vision pierced and rent it and shook the earth with its sudden interruption. *Quickly, quickly, before they disappear forever!* The portal to the world of the gods was shifting, narrowing, shrinking, squeezing itself into a soft tunnel that would perhaps empty into more welcoming hands than the ones that she happened to bear. Without blinking, without thinking, she pulled the jewels from their palanquin of air and flung them upon the emerald grass, where they immediately broke into a waterfall of crystalline shards.

She was startled, but she was not alarmed. She viewed the scene before her as if through a prism. Even the way the pieces burst out in all directions was delightful, not unpleasant to the senses. At that moment, she was able to see herself not merely as a being acting alone on the basis of blind impulse. Rather, every small occurrence that had led her here, from the passage through that moldering tunnel all the way back to the trial and verdict of the Old Ones, shined before her like the light of sprites upon a darkened footpath of many stones, illuminated one by one.

She was the weaver, and here was her loom. She could unravel whatever elements she didn't see fit to intertwine with the others. She could add another if she found anything at all lacking in her warp and weft. And with this excruciatingly precise motion, she would see to it that the world could inch forward, slowly but surely. But she could not simply attribute this activity to the delusion of a destiny made for her alone. She was but one of the threads, looped over others, and still more others.

I alone am not responsible for this. This is also the doing of the Old Ones.

She closed her eyes and felt the souls of the three jewels soar heavenward, twirling figures disappearing in a trail of clouds, before they joined together in a diadem of dark light and arced back to her. In a motion that resembled the strike of a match against a wall of night, the three jewels fused into a single face of winking fire and wavering rune before they pierced her heart. The pain was that of a dozen swords slicing into thick and fibrous flesh; it was a pain of blood, bubbles, heat, and an ancient secrecy rent to pieces by the holy soul of curiosity.

We know you, we see you, and thus, you must not conceal yourself. She could hear them, voices of air and salt that bulged beneath the tides of her skin.

With that, the green field around her faded into a watery mist. The two roads before her were gone, although she knew in her heart that she had already chosen. She was back in the cave, knee-deep in a gully of cool water. But she knew she was not alone. As the spirits of the unsleeping spiraled like petals in a wild wind around her, she closed her eyes and saw another vision.

She wore a long vermilion gown, which fluttered poppy-like on a mountain breeze. The fragrance of incense filled the sky, and women's melodic voices floated on high like balloons to a cathedral ceiling. Ahead of her, on a grassy knoll, she saw the three jewels, but they were merely faceless figures robed in white, each of them holding a chalice of colored fire.

You have not yet been received by your destiny, they whispered to her. *Open your eyes and look.*

She broke from her reverie, opened her eyes, and strained her vision across the inky tunnel so that she could see the barely perceptible light perched upon a rivet in some far-off cave. But as she kept looking, she did not see endless sheets of rock, branch, and pit. She herself was a breathing and sentient organ aware of her placement against the spine of a larger living being. For the first time, she felt gratitude for all the forces seen and unseen that had nudged her forward, slid her down the chute of this peculiar journey.

She swam, faster and faster, until she could almost touch the light. *Could it be . . . the jewels?* She reached forward tentatively, wondering what they would be like as realities birthed from her strange visions. But no, what she had seen from so far away was not the jewels at all.

We are the origin, the primal clay of your world. From now on, you will be so close to us, you will no longer view us as separate from you. This is a great fortune and also a great danger, as it is the manner whereby your kind forget their own divinity. Touch your hand to the place where we rest, and recall others to this simple gesture, for it will remind you that we are never far, that we are bound and indebted to you just as you are to us.

She floated noiselessly in the water and touched her palm to her throbbing heart, which was beating out a cadence of sorrow, of liquid light, of tears, of spring blooms, of aching, of bitter wormwood, of the transcendent suffering that funnels from root to crown. She did not know if she could bear the journey any longer. Silt slipped through her toes, and she could feel her body becoming heavier and heavier, but still, she was held there, entranced by the sight before her.

They rested on an embankment of sludge and water-softened stone: a rosebush levitating upon a puff of smoke; an olive tree that rained down a small waterfall of slick, apple-colored oil; and a sheaf of waving golden wheat sprouting alongside a large and warmly scented loaf of bread.

She hesitated to draw closer, but she was filled with the rage of hunger. She paddled across the last stretch of water, and unheeding of her wetness, her nakedness, she seized the loaf of bread and dipped it in the waterfall of oil. Not questioning the strange and sudden nature of these apparitions, she tore off a hunk of the loaf and stuffed it in her mouth. It was the most delicious food she had ever tasted. She felt the exertion of the men and women in the olive groves, crushing the olives into a fine paste to produce the delectable extract. And as her teeth tore through the bread, she could almost feel sunlight bursting through the golden heads of wheat, dancing and bobbing in the wind.

As she breathed in the pure and full scent of the rose, so shameless and sensual, she knew that her hand had exacted a price. These three things before her were gifts, but they were also messages. She looked down and saw that she was no longer naked. She was robed in a sarong of swirling red. No longer untouched and no longer the same. The voice that poured out of her was so foreign, she didn't know if it was her own or that of the jewels.

Another sound erupted from across the stony bank. She looked, and there it was! A beautiful mare, red-brown, with a diamond of white upon its brow. The mare whinnied and reared and tossed back her mane and regarded the woman with eyes luminous and knowing. Like the rosebush, the olive tree, and the waving sheaves of wheat, the horse was encircled in a halo of golden light. The woman approached, and the mare regarded her with either indifference or vague acknowledgment, as if she were an old but quite expected friend. Tentatively, the woman patted her on her forelock, and the mare bowed, exposing a back covered by a shimmering golden saddle.

The woman recognized this was all part of her anointment.

She touched her face softly to the mare's muzzle and breathed in the sweetness of this creature. From where had she come? Despite the question that buzzed beneath her skin, the woman felt as if she were being cautioned not to deliberate overmuch on the mare's mysterious appearance. Before them was neither grass nor water, nor was there any sign of a pasture. Even here, even in the soft, pale cave-light shed by the gifts before her, she felt entirely in the custody of some titanic monster of the netherworld. A tug of familiar bitterness came over her. Was she alone, after all? Was there no way out?

She touched the place over her heart and felt three beads of heat come into her fingers. At the same time, the wraiths that had followed her so steadfastly swirled around her in a cold cyclone of phantom limbs.

Mount the horse.

It was not the three jewels who had spoken, nor was it the faceless specters. What she heard was the sound of her own voice. It did not still her beating heart, but this was the reality she had birthed — one in which the lack of solace would reveal a new world that would not be created by will alone.

But could she have faith in the invisible when she did not know where she was going?

Mount the horse.

She steadied herself and climbed upon the saddle. Again, the mare whinnied and reared, and the woman felt an overwhelming nausea as they sped into the darkness. She looked behind her and saw nothing but a puff of smoke where the rosebush, the olive tree, and the sheaves of wheat had been.

Go toward the Hall of Dreams. This is the destruction of time.

She didn't know how she knew, but as the mare raced across a bridge of icy stalagmites, the woman remembered tales of the Hall of Dreams—from a time long before she'd come to believe that the cerulean skies and endless song of such a place was just another sweet figment, quelled by the cloak of storm and repentance that the Old Ones had thrown over all things living.

The mare galloped on until everything around the woman was a dim and billowy sheet of faces and memories. One particular memory stood out. She was a child, and a large red balloon had just landed in the midst of a glade. She was running toward it. Her mother called out to her to stop — she might hurt herself. She was running so quickly that everything was blue, green, alternating wisps of cool darkness. Her happiness was one of agitation, a quickening of her pulse that wanted no boundaries. As she fell and skinned her knees upon the earth, that was the very instant the balloon docked in the grass.

Now also, she recalled the fever dreams of her youth, after the war, when she was struck by visions of the ocean. Everyone thought she would surely die, and she could do nothing but stay in bed while her mother wept softly or prayed in the next room. She felt feeble and full of failure. And the sea was in her dream — here, here, and she knew not where. But it kept coming to her, through the blackness of night, coming to her in its entirety even though she had never seen it, never known it. The entire essence of the sea was in her, and she grasped it in her illness. Such a calmness, such a sureness of possession that she would never feel again. Never, never, never.

Such strange thoughts, things she hadn't imagined or felt or sensed in years, came to her like that. Across the bridges of rock, the mare galloped, into a place where there was no more gravity, but only a menagerie of hazy objects and faces falling through the rubble of space. All around her, the air was brittle. Melting clocks and solemn men with gray beards floated in a soup of starry mist.

She clutched the mare's mane even though there was nothing around her — no wind, no elements. She recollected the matron deity of her family, a woman with a hideous aspect, claws and tusks, ashen face smeared with blood, and bright, all-seeing eyes. Regeneration, revenge, fear, dark magic, and dark thoughts were her terrain.

In her dreams when the woman was younger, there was always an old woman ahead of her on a journey, and there was always an old woman behind her too, and they were not necessarily the same and could sometimes be fearful or kindly, dangerous or delightful. She did not know where this old woman came from; perhaps she was merely given to her by her family, and there was no choice in the matter.

And though everything was approaching chaos in this place that was not a where, there still seemed to be a road made of cave rock, and the mare glided on, past the mangroves, the bits of fabric that blossomed out into a spray of meaningless foliage, the melting clocks, the sad and wizened beings who drifted noiselessly past.

Then, the cave road approached what appeared to be a cliff edge, and the woman, too, began to feel herself floating down, but now, she was not any where in particular at all.

She was in a soft vortex of stars. And she did not know how she knew, but as she held her fingers to her heart and breathed in the gauzy softness, she was aware that she had come to the birthplace of the gods. And that she had carried all the souls of those fallen warriors who had kept vigil over her.

The Overworld. This is the where that exists after death, when time is no more, and gods go to be reborn.

And the old woman she had seen in the dreams of her youth, whom she knew to be some primeval aspect of a god who never died or changed its form, reappeared before her, turned around. She wasn't hideous at all. She simply had no face. There was only darkness. And stars.

The woman closed her eyes, and indeed, time was nothing but an intake of air before its inevitable expulsion. All was still, quiet. When she opened her eyes, she was in a familiar knoll. It was not beautiful, but ravaged, the carpet of grass strewn with burn marks, as if a great battle had been waged and all signs of life shorn from the earth itself. There was a clocktower—how familiar yet how long ago!— once lovely and resonant, but now mottled by time and disuse, its bulbous bell rusted and heavy. The windows were a sad arrangement of broken teeth.

As she came closer, she could see that she was not in a majestic place. But all the same, as she and the mare trotted slowly toward the clocktower, a small cluster of people—wee ones and elderfolk alike— approached her. She shuddered in antici- pation of sticks, stones, bones, rotted meat hurled at her, as this had been the customary greeting of villagers from the lowlands and highlands alike. Momentarily, she felt naked without her old armor, but the cool breeze on her skin and the way her hair floated like a dark cloud, buoyed by lightning, across her bare shoulders filled her with a serenity she had nearly forgotten.

The looks on the dirty faces before her were neither ugly nor filled with spit and bile. They gazed at her with a wondrous recognition, as if she were someone they had not only been expecting, but eagerly awaiting. A small, plump wee one with a long dark braid and a scarlet cloak embroidered with gold skipped toward her and looked up, eyes glazed with awe, holding forth a clump of dewy mountain flowers, white and fragrant.

The woman took the modest bouquet and breathed it in. All she could do was weep—in remembrance of what had come before and in heartbroken astonishment at the sheer unknown of the present and future. As she wept, the village folk surrounded her. The wee ones nuzzled the beautiful mare and shyly regarded the woman, while the elderfolk lifted her gently off the horse and offered her many tokens of their welcome: large stone goblets of apple wine, bowls of corn porridge, spongey towers of lentil cake, handfuls of nuts and crumbled cheese. She ate and ate, and it was just as delicious as the food from the cave — full of the dark soil of earth and the golden sunlight that had beaten down upon the men and women who turned the hand cranks, fermented the lentils, picked the fruit, milked the cows, and ground the corn into a fine, sweet paste.

She passed the time there, in the circle of caring attendants. She learned that the Old Ones were gone. For how long, she could not be certain — the language in which the villagers spoke was strange liquid silver, lovely and overflowing, and although she could ascertain some words here and there, as well as features

upon faces that reminded her of her dear mam and others she had once known, she had not been the only one transformed by her passage to other lands. She knew enough to be sure that the ones here now were the ones who had been awaiting her for countless epochs, the ones who had prophesied the light of a blood moon — a moon that glowed upon all the earth's inhabitants, damned and blessed alike. As they looked upon her with all their questions and all their yearning, she thought her heart would break.

She pointed to it and said, "This is the seed. Here, everything grows before it takes root in the world we see. But in order to reap the fruits of our gift, we must build new temples to honor new gods — gods who are just as alive and passionate as we, who do not live in distant realms but in our own wisdom and love. And just as the earth nourishes and clothes us like a doting mother, we too must nourish and clothe our dead through sacrament and remembrance. Thus, our temples to the gods will also be temples to the spirits; our honor shall bring them great auspiciousness in the Overworld. All will be mourned and celebrated in like fashion so that those who did not enjoy peace and the love of their neighbors on earth will find restitution in the heavens."

Altogether, in that dark place, their hearts bowed before the altar of the moment, and it did not matter that they were in a barren, broken scape in which the arcana of yesteryear loomed heavy above everything else. They looked to her for more answers, but she only smiled and said, "Love is the law of this land. Come, there is much work to be done."

The story has been told for all time, at least the time we know so well. There are many versions of it. Some say the woman was a goddess who had been sent to the people to cleanse them of the terror left in the Old Ones' wake, to bring innocence back to the land. Some say that when the woman approached, with her unearthly gentleness and her graceful mare, she was naked and enshrouded in flames, although her flesh remained unscathed. Some say this was so, yet her love for her people eventually turned her mortal.

One thing remains constant in all tellings of the tale; as soon as the tears from her eyes fell upon the ground—alighting in that land where little was said to take hold in the fallow earth — a rosebush, an olive tree, and a field of wheat sprang up. It is believed that they continue to grow, to this very day.

www.ingramcontent.com/pod-product-compliance
Lightning Source LLC
Chambersburg PA
CBHW040912010826

48978CB00013BB/1252